The Heart Shape...
Where is it from?

By Inna Geim

The heart shape...
Where is it from?

Copyright @Inna Geim, 2024

Contact info: innachon2@yahoo.com
First published in the USA in 2024
Publisher: Feet Balance Orthotics LLC
ISBN number: 978–1–947142–12–1
Cover/Interior design by Inna Chon
Illustrations by Inna Chon

Table of contents

The heart shape...
Where is it from?

The heart shape . . .
The universal shape representing "Love."

Is anyone on this earth doesn't know about this sweet shape?

1

Ubiquitous... all over the world.
Just seeing or drawing this shape softens and warms our hearts.

We all seek love . . . wanting to love and being loved. Who doesn't want to be loved and to love?

Because our hearts are meant to be filled with love. The hearts filled with love completes our being and drives out fear.

Love sounds soft and cozy, but so powerful and never dies. It makes things better and covers every fault. Even after we are gone, it still lives in other people's heart who received our love. This heart shape has that power.

People use this heart shape just for decorations too.

Small and big, plump and slender, fancy and simple of this heart shape...

People make heart shape everywhere.
On the walls, fabrics, trees, goods and stuffs...

Drawing it, carving it, weaving it, forging it together with things...

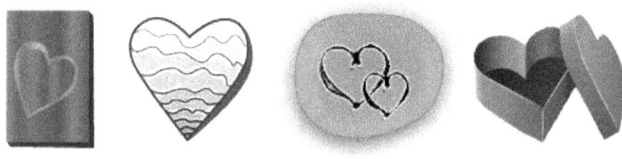

When filled with color, it's either red or pink...

Why...? Why not yellow, blue or orange... Or any other color...?

I love drawing heart shapes... like some people do.

One day while drawing all different heart shapes on a paper just to kill time...

Hmmm... curious... I became.

Where did this heart shape come from...?

Who designed it...
When did people start using this heart shape...?

Some say it's from the shape of our heart in our chest, the organ heart...

Really...? I looked into it . . . the shape of the heart in our chest.

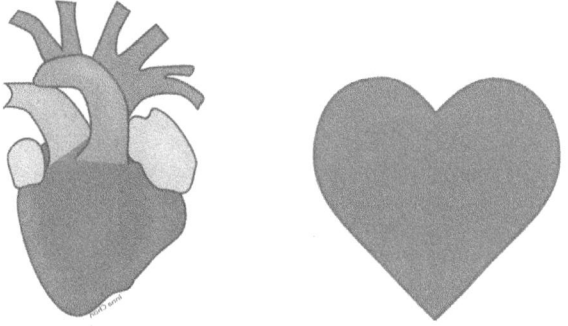

The one on the left is an extremely simplified drawing of the organ heart shape with extremely simplified color scheme.

The one on the right is the typical heart shape that represents love in our heart.

So, we have two hearts in us...

The organ heart in our chest is the engine for our physical body keeps pumping, and it needs oxygen and food to function properly. One day, it would stop beating and becomes dust.

The other heart, the invisible one in us, is the engine for our soul, mind, and spirit that cannot be touched, though that heart forms who we really are. And it needs to fill with love to function properly... if not, it shrinks and would not function properly. That means our soul, mind, and spirit cannot function properly.

So, one heart for the hardware and another heart for the software...

I don't see any resemblance between the two. Do you...?

The love heart shape is not from the organ heart shape. No, I don't think so.

This started my journey in search for the origin of the heart shape that represents love that has a power to change people's hearts...

I googled it, the old Asian symbols, letters, and characters...

Among Asian Hebrews…

I didn't see it…

Among Egyptian hieroglyphs…

I didn't find it.

Among Chinese characters…?

激情的形状从何而来心水土壤
空气精神上帝眼睛嘴巴人类物
鼻子船小大中高低窄魂...

No, wasn't there.
I checked on the Internet for other old characters… and surprised to see there are so many I have never heard of.

Pictish alphabets with all that swirling could have had come up with one... at least with a similar heart shape.

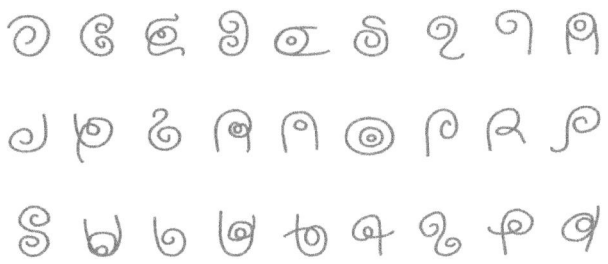

But hadn't.

Phoenician, Chaldean, Greek, Magi, Theban, Demotic...

Malachim of sticks and tiny circles,

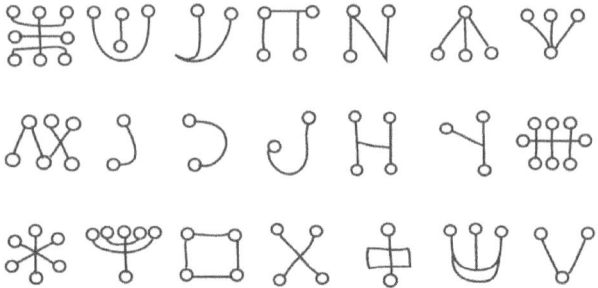

 Tangwar, Futhark, Celestial... Etc., etc.

There wasn't a shape that resembles the heart shape—even a little...!

Human is a creative being, though, among all those shapes humans had created for their letters or symbols for thousands of years didn't include this heart shape...

Seriously, "No."

No one came up with the heart shape that represents "Love."

Now, try finding love shape in nature. One says the heart shape is from the shape of the bleeding-heart flower.

However, though the creator, God made the flower shape that amazingly depicts the heart that bleeds, the flower itself has nothing to do with love. It just resembles the heart shape. So, the heart shape didn't come from this flower.

Other sources say different things with the similar shapes, but not clear in its explanation in connection with the love we feel with the heart shape we talk about.

Even, some say, the heart shape was on an ancient coin, but that shape is not exactly the heart shape and didn't represent love.

This heart shape didn't evolve from some other shapes, from the get-go, the heart shape was the heart shape as we know… We just draw them thinner or fatter.

So, there got to be a clear one original source.

Then where did it come from…?

Curiosity... swelling...

I decided to ask God, who knows everything.

Whenever I use the heart shape expressing my love for whomever, whatever... and whenever it popped in my mind...

While driving, walking, cooking...

Persistently...
Thankfully, that I am kind of a persistent person.

Asked I...

"Father God, where did this heart shape come from? "

"Who designed it?"
"When did we start using it...?"

Weeks past...
Months past...
A year passed by...

Seriously, no answer...!!?

Very unusual... God usually doesn't delay
this long...

Still persistent was I.
I knew he knows... for sure.
God knows everything
He's omniscient.

More than a few times, I play whining;
"Daddy, aren't you tired of me whining and whining about this...? Where is it from...? Please . . ."

Still no answer, no inspiration.

Almost a couple years past, and I wasn't asking as often as before, but whenever it pops in my mind asked why... still persistence in play.

You know, persistence, never fails...
After all, isn't persistence one of the important ingredient of love . . .?

Finally... a little after a couple of years—I thought after God tested my persistence out—one Sunday morning, as usual, I was sitting at the church, listening the pastor.

He was preaching about God being 'the Way, the Truth, and the Life."

Who doesn't know that phrase...?
But that day, then, there, the word "Life" caught my attention, and my brain started spinning.

Yes, God is Life—the Author of Life.
Everything with life in it moves.
If it's full of life, it moves freely and fast.

I wasn't listening the pastor. I was totally zoned out.

Ok, then which shape can move most freely and fastest...? It's got to be a BALL...!

19

The "Ball shape" in three-dimensional space.

Yes, that is why God made everything with the ball shape.

All those humongous planets are all in the ball shape and all the way down to the atoms, the smallest of the element... we cannot see with naked eyes: protons, neutrons, and electrons are all in nano tiny ball shapes... and spinning like crazy...

Who knows how fast they spin?
Full of life…!!

So, if we got to pick an earthly shape that represents God in two dimensional… Obviously…

It's got to be a circle, a round shape… with a full life in it. And for the life on earth, it has to have blood—red blood. The earthly life sustained by the blood. As God said,

"the life of the flesh is in the blood." (Leviticus 17:11)
Wherever blood goes, it heals.

This circle that represents God is supple with life in it... not hard at all.
And a spear pokes it...

And through it pierces this circle shape... with life in it.

Yes, the blood was shed and made the perfect heart shape, isn't it?

Yes, that was the answer to me. This heart shape was made... from God being pierced...

Of course, every good thing is from God...

While He is being pierced... He created the heart shape.

So, heart shape represents the "Pierced God...!"

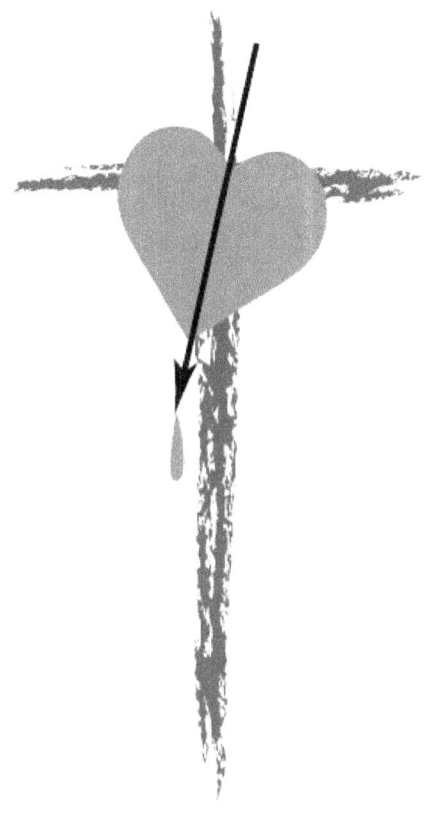

On that day, 2000 years ago, God showed his love for us when Jesus, God in flesh, was pierced by a spear on that cross, shedding his blood to pay for the wage of our sins, the death.

The death paid by a Death. And God did it for us to bring us back to life—to Himself.

That is why the heart shape should be filled with red, the color of the blood, the life.

And why pink…?

Mix the red blood and white that represents Jesus' holiness, purity, sinless nature as God…

Here we go… the "Pink…"

That is why the original colors of the heart just have to be red or pink…

Isn't it so logical…! To me, it was…! That's it…!!!

All this happened because "God Loves us."

All this went through my brain for about 5 minutes or so… my curiosity over the origine of the heart shape for over two years ended in just 5 minutes . . . on that Sunday while listing the sermon about the words, "God is the Way, the Truth, and the Life."

The heart shape that represents love is made when God in flesh, Jesus, got pierced because of His love for us—while we were still sinners, unlovable.

Yes, God is the expert in creating wonderous things—always with life in it—even with the broken stuffs.

I think after Jesus was pierced, God revealed the heart shape to someone and it started to circulate.

We will find out in heaven when and to whom God revealed this heart shape.

Because in heaven, everything will be revealed… Everything…!

God has a way to keep the records all that have happened since the creation.
Oh, but don't worry about our sinful acts at all, because we are all squeaky clean, and all will be understood and will understand.

Isn't it exciting…?

Think about… God … the awesome God…!!!
How can we express God properly with earthly words? And He loves us, the sinners, who were on the death row, so much… and

came to the death row to rescue us...! And rescued me...!!

I just love Him so much...!!!

I am very satisfied with the answer to my question, "The heart shape, where is it from...?"

So, I wanted to share with you.

Then What is "Love?"

Then what is "Love?" We all have different ideas of love, and there are different loves: romantic love between men & women, parental love between parents and children, love between friends.

Many philosophers and religions described love. But not clearly.

But the Bible—the instruction manual from the Manufacturer of mankind, our God—speaks often about love. One verse that deeply resonates with me is: *'Love covers many things.'* To me, it's similar to the saying, *'Love is blind.'*

I loved my husband so much that I couldn't see the truth—that he had some narcissistic traits—for 42 years...!!! My humongous love was covering all his flaws.

I had no idea what I was really dealing with—I was simply happy.

God really showed me how love covers many things. Or, maybe, God kept providing me with the love to love him. Anyhow, through it all, I became as strong, patient, and resilient as I could be—I just thank God for all that traits I collected going through my life loving all kinds of people around me.

You know best thing people say when leaving you or leaving this earth is, "I loved you." And this saying covers whatever happened in their relationship. But imagine if someone, after whatever good they had done, saying, "I have never loved you." That kills everything. Isn't it?

Love has that much power: Power to lift you to the moon and power to deflate you to bottom.

Anyway, that saying, "Love covers many things" was both in the Old Testament and New Testament.

In the Old Testament, in the book of Proverbs chapter 10, verse 12, the King Solomon, known as the wisest man on earth 3,000 years ago, wrote, "Hatred stirs up strife, but *love covers all sins."*

And 2000 years ago, Peter, one of the 12 disciples of Jesus wrote in the New Testament, 1 Peter 4:8 says, "Love covers multitude of sins."

Also, Solomon says in the book of Song of Songs in chapter 8, verse 6, "Love is as strong as death."

Yes, when you truly love someone, you'd even be willing to die for them. And the love of a parent is often so strong, they would lay down their life for their children. That is what our Heavenly Father did for us.

Yet, most of us do not know what the true love really means, though we all want to love and be loved with the true love—the love that originated from God.

There are lots of explanations about love, from philosophers, religions, but not clearly as in the Instruction, the Bible.

In New Testament, 1 Corinthian chapter 13, known as the lover chapter, verses from 4-7, the Apostle Paul wrote;

"Love is patient, love is kind. It does not envy, it does not boast, it is not proud. It does not dishonor others, it is not self-seeking, it is not easily angered, it keeps no record of wrongs. Love does not delight in evil but rejoices with the truth. It always protects, always trusts, always hopes, always perseveres."

Isn't it interesting? The love starts with patience and ends with perseverance.

This means if you love someone, you never give up...!

And the verse 8 starts with, "Love never fails."

Of course, you don't give up, you cannot fail.

I summed up all the above explanation of love: it covers all things, strong as death, patient, kind, not envying, not boasting, not proud, not dishonor others, not self-seeking, not easily angered, keeps no record of wrongs, not delight in evil, rejoices with the truth, always protects, always trusts, always hopes, always perseveres...

Sounds very invincible... With all those ingredients. True love cannot be defeated...! That was the love I was getting from my Father in Heaven.

People doing things with love stand strong, whatever happens. So, love should be at the hub of every good thing we do.

Think about someone doing all kinds of good things; even doing their best... but without love, they are doing them out of their pride, the core trait of Satan.

When things go wrong, they become undone. Because pride is weak and fragile.

This makes the opposite of love the pride, not hate…!

In Old Testament, Solomon says in the book Proverbs chapter 16, verse 18 says, "Pride comes before destruction, a haughty spirit before a fall."

How all that Happened...?

My thoughts here. If you truly love somebody, you become creative to make that someone happy.

Out of love, God wanted to create mankind, us, in His image, that was Jesus, one of the characters of God's trinity that has an image.

God Himself is described as pure, radiant light with all powerful energy we cannot even imagine in it—too powerful for our earthly bodies to withstand. If we were to encounter Him directly, our body would be consumed by His brilliance.

Holy spirit is a spirit... no image. This holy spirit deciphers and interprets God's power and His characters.

Jesus is the only one with an image of heavenly body that contains God and Holy Spirit and carries out God's characters and plans with heavenly beings.

They are separate but together. It's like we have spirit, mind, and body.

I will find out when I go to heaven. Because, in heaven, everything will be revealed.

And God wants to create mankind in His image, so we are created. (Genesis 1:26-27)

As we are created in Jesus's image, and we inviting God and Holy Spirit into us would transform us more like Jesus in our earthly body.

Anyways, the purpose of God creating mankind was to have a relationship, a loving Father and children relationship.

That is why before God created us, He prepared everything for us in advance, just as any loving, capable parent would do. Of course, it's done in God's scale.

God created the earth with a perfect system that can provide us with everything we need. All of them beautifully with seeds in them so the cycle of life continues with their own certain period . . . producing what we need season after season.

There God prepared a nursery room, the Garden of Eden with many trees that are pleasing to the eyes and good for food for the mankind, His children. The ground was kept soft and moist by mist coming up from the earth; so mankind can walk around freely with bare feet in comfort and delight enjoying and taking care of the garden.

After all this, God created Adam and Eve, our ancestors, with a will to choose. It was the risky but necessary thing for God. Without the will to choose, we would be like robots, then God's intended genuine love relationship would not be possible. And God gave the entire earth with everything in it to Adam and Eve, to us.
Here is the thing about relationships . . .

Every relationship establishes and thrives with give and take. One person always giving but not receiving anything is not a healthy relationship. That kind of relationship won't last long.

God knew. So God even provided something for mankind to give back to God. That is where the "Tree of Knowledge of Good and Evil" comes in.

God puts the tree in the middle of the Garden with so many other trees—the trees that were beautiful to look at and good for food—freely given for mankind's enjoyment.

It's like God wants the mankind to see the tree easily and remember Him that all the things are from God.

And God told them not to eat from that tree—from only one tree, and warned them, "If you eat from it, you will certainly die." the law, the command of God. In the beginning, there was only one law, one command. How simple, how clear, and how easy it was to follow!

I don't know if mankind understood what is dying, or death meant. Though whether they fully understood death or not, the meaning was clear—this tree's fruits belonged to God alone.

That makes the tree, the tree of knowledge of good and evil, the only thing that mankind could express their gratitude, thankfulness, appreciation, respect to God for giving everything by just not eating from the tree.

They still could enjoy admiring the tree and have nice time under the tree while munching and sharing so many of other fruits from all the other different trees.

I looked up the name of the tree—the Tree of Knowledge of Good and Evil—in the Hebrew text. And found it has a deeper meaning of "A source of understanding that encompasses both moral rightness and wrongness. It signifies the capacity to discern between what is considered ethically acceptable and unacceptable."

It talks about moral and ethics.

It's hard for me to grasp the condition of mankind's cognitive status before they ate the forbidden fruit. But I imagine it they must have had pure consciousness, pure intelligence, pure trust; so, no doubt, no judgement, no shame of any kind.

Hence the life in the garden must have been like a life in Heaven—Heaven on earth with God there waking and talking with mankind. And I think the God who talked and walked in the garden was Jesus in His heavenly body.

By the way, what a life in the Garden of Eden be...!! Mankind enjoying delicious 100% organic food and a beautiful dwelling place — no rent, no payment. Their only payment was not eating the fruit from the tree.

But they reach out and ate it...!

It wasn't a mistake, or no one shoved it into their mouths. They knew they shouldn't... but when the father of lies, the hater of God, coaxed them with lies, they listened that liar and reached out their hands, and took it, and ate it.

I thought about the lie the serpent said. The serpent started with a twisted question about eating, planting doubt. Then he lied outright about the consequence of eating the fruit.

God said, "You will certainly die." But the serpent added a word "Not" and changed the word, "Certainly" to "Surely."

The difference of these two words? I researched the meanings in Hebrew words and found the Hebrew word used for "Certainly" carries a stronger and more absolute meaning than the Hebrew word used for "surely." And by saying that, the serpent, the original narcissist, portrayed God as a liar...!! The original narcissist twisted truth into deception.

As a result, the God's word of consequence of eating the fruit "You will certain die" became "You will Not surely die." And then the serpent said, "Your eyes will be opened, and you will be like God, knowing good and evil," which ended up to be true. But that truth became the snare that doomed mankind to hell—the death, the eternal separation from God.

This act of sin—an utterly selfish and greedy act of taking the only one thing that belonged to God while already having everything— placed mankind under the father of lies' control.

Now, humanity was shackled to the father of lies who schemes to drag us with him into forever hell where he can torment the very mankind that God created to love, with unspeakable hideous ways . . . forever.

It's like people lying about drugs these days. We all know the drugs certainly damage the brain and destroy health. But the lie is told, "Drugs will surely not harm you—just take them, and the realities disappear and you will be happy." And most people do that not realizing that the so-called happiness is nothing more than their brain malfunctioning, creating illusions.

When you think about, no other creatures knowingly do something harmful to themselves. Only humans do. Not just what they put into their mouth, but also the words they use, and even playing dangerous things— like boxing, where hitting each other's heads.

The head is the software of our body machine and cannot be replaced. Why let someone hit your head...!?

You won't let anyone hit the software of their computer even though that can be replaced.

We know the drugs and smoking are harmful, and foul languages are destructive. But humans still use them with their own mouths. Ironically most of times to justify themselves oblivious of the foul languages prove the opposite of what they want to achieve. Because the words that come out of their mouth define who they are.

Also, humans are so prone to believe lies. The biggest outright lie of all is the evolution theory. Evolution is the process of things grow from the seeds to adult. God put seeds in every creatures and all seeds are programmed to grow with certain steps evolving from one stage to the next stage until they reach their full growth.

If the evolution theory is true, there got to be some creatures in between—still evolving. But there is none. There is no creature of half monkey and half human. Even fruit flies won't evolve to even a smallest whatever the regular flies even if we give them for 1,000 years . . . even the shape of wings would not change a bit.

And people say that is the missing link...! This is the proof how profoundly dumb and imbecilic humans can become if they don't believe and follow the instruction manual from the human manufacturer, God, the Bible.

And schools that supposed to teach truth teach that big outright lie and people pay big money for that too... utterly idiotic and moronic...!!

Anyways, I thought about how it would have had felt for God when He saw the mankind eating the fruits and joined the father of lies.

Let's say you are so rich and generous. And found a friend who has nothing. And you decided to help him providing for everything he needs: food, a house, clothes, everything. And out of kindness, you even think, "Maybe, he would like to show gratitude toward me by giving something." But since he has nothing to give, you hand him $10 saying, "Use this to buy me something small for my birthday."

Later you found, your friend used the money for himself—on something you provided him abundantly already...! On top of that, he was sided with someone who hates you.

How would you feel...? I would feel really hurt, disappointed, and betrayed. That's how mankind chose to betray God with their will.

Now what?

Should God have just forgiven mankind? Because God is love? But God is also righteous and holy. A holy God cannot dwell with someone who committed sin. Righteous God cannot overlook unrighteousness.

As a result, mankind ended up dying as God had warned. Here, dying means complete separation from life—God.

Here on earth, as long as we breathe, we have life. But when our breathing stops, our earthly body ceases to function, and our soul leaves our body, and goes either to heaven or hell and lives forever.

However, it wasn't a sudden death. God in His mercy provided time for mankind to repent. A sudden death would have left mankind with no chance to repent and turn back to Him.

Instead, God cursed the ground and make the ground produce thorns and thistles. And God said there will be pain; very severe pain for Eve when delivering a baby and Adam will eat from painful toil (Genesis 3:16-19), and God sent Adam out of the Garden of Eden—you don't pay, you get evicted.

Now, the ground would no longer keep its softness by itself. As a result, to grow food, Adam to till the ground to soften the soil while walking and living on the cursed ground dealing with thorns and thistles as well.

Also, Adam's growing family kept walking on the ground hardening and flattening the soil gradually little by little.

If you know the human foot structure with an arch at the bottom, the actual foundation our body, and it is formed by tarsal joint, a group of 20 tiny joints that meant to be supported by the soft soil to keep the joints from falling, you would understand how walking on flattening ground would make the tarsal joint to fall and tilt the anklebones where our body stands and puts our entire body out of alignment. These tilted anklebones guarantee the pain in the major joints and feet if not now, later on. I am sure that contributed to the painful life.

Anyhow, surely, the pain would have had reminded Adam and Eve of their sin and stirred sorrow in their hearts. I believe Adam and Eve have had repented and shared their story again and again with their offsprings reminding them to remember God and bring offerings to Him. Because that was what they withheld—the fruits of the tree of knowledge of good and evil—that led them their fall.

Adam who was created to live forever died at the age of 930 years old living on the cursed ground ... with pain.

As time passed by, after Adam's death, less and less people remember Adam's teaching of remembering God. And by the time of Noah, he was the only one who remembered God. The entire population on the earth became so wicked, evil, violent, and corrupt—except Noah. (Genesis 6:5-13)

God's heart troubled deeply to the point of wiping out the entire population back then, except Noah's family. Now, with one family, God's plan to have loving relationship with mankind continues.

I am sure Noah did his best to teach his family and his descendants about God and to remember Him until his death at the age of 950.

Over the years, as Noah's descendants multiplied, they built a city with a tower that they thought to reach the heavens, and they wanted to stick together not scattering over the earth. But it wasn't God's plan. God created the earth beautifully for mankind to fill and enjoy, not to huddle in one corner.

Up to that point, people spoke only one language. And God said, "With one language humans begun to do this. Then nothing they plan to do will be impossible to them."

I agree, especially, with humans' inclination to ignore and rebel against God.

Thus, God confused their language. As a result, they all babbled, so they couldn't understand each other. Consequently, the communication cut off, without communication couldn't continue working together. So stopped the project of building the tower and gained the name of tower as "The Tower of Babel."

Eventually, people separated by different languages and into different nations.

And during Noah's 10th generation, God called Abram, a son of Terah who worshiped other gods (Joshua 24:2), and told him to leave his home country to where God will show him.

Without knowing where God would lead him, Abram obeyed, and years later, even to the point of sacrificing Issac, his only son with his beloved wife Sarah, trusting God. I cannot imagine what went through Abraham's mind in the moment he lifted the knife over Issac and Issac's mind watching his father lifting the knife over his bound body—whew…!!

And, eventually, through Abraham's grandson, Jacob, came Israelites.

Again, I am sure that Abraham and Jacob taught their descendants about God. Yet, as before, people forgot Him and become rebellious once again.

But God had a plan—a plan to bring us back to Him. Because we are His creation, and He still loves us.

For that to happen, a righteous God had to deal with the wedge of our sin fairly and justly. How…? By dying for us—taking our place. By the death—painful physical death, that we ourselves had brought upon humanity by disobeying God's command.

Out of love for us, God came down, this time, in flesh, in earthly body, just like us. That was Jesus, God in flesh.

God coming down in flesh served two purposes. First, to reveal Himself—the Way, the Truth, and the Life—to us in such a loving and caring way . . . feeding the hungry, healing the sick, and forgiving sinners, and walking among us. Second, to use the earthly body to pay for our debt—the death we owed.

After showing us who He is, teaching us His way, Jesus— our savior, fully God and fully human—carried the cross to where the debt had paid fully—for all our sins; the previous sins, ongoing sins, and future sins for the entire mankind on the whole earth . . . by the death . . . in the most painful way of death . . . on that cross. There He said, "It is all finished." There Jesus completed His mission to bring us back.

There has never been a mission greater than this in all of our history—one that shook both heaven and earth.

God didn't use any of His power to lessen the pain inflicted on Him. God bore it fully, satisfyingly the claim of the debtor—the serpent, the Satan, the father of lies—who was entitled to take sinners to hell—the place you want to die but cannot die, cannot escape—that is the hell, the place where Satan delights in torturing lost souls forever and ever.

Know that when Jesus died to pay for our sins, He did it with His authority, and Jesus came back to life, because He is the Life itself—the very Author of Life.

The 12 disciples whom Jesus prepared were to spread the Good News:

"For God so loved the world, that he gave his only begotten Son, that whosoever believes in him should not perish, but have everlasting life." (John 3:16).

At first, the disciples had hard time understanding what Jesus was saying. Because disciples were talking about the earthly things and earthly kingdom that won't last forever, and Jesus was talking about heavenly things and heavenly kingdom that lasts forever.

For a while, the conversations between Jesus and His disciples ran in parallel. It took three years for disciples understand what Jesus was saying with the help of all the prophesies about Jesus in the Old Testament.

Then Jesus ascended back up to heaven promising to come back to take us with Him.

Afterward, the disciples were baptized with holy spirit and went about to share the good news. And what happened to the disciples? While spreading the good news, most of them had been murdered.

Yet, their story didn't end in tragedy. The sure thing is they are all in heaven living with God with no more pain, no more tears. They basically all retired fairly at young ages, because they had that free insurance that guarantees when their souls leave the earthly body, they start living the heavenly retirement life forever.

If there is no heaven & hell, then truly most pitiful people would be the disciples and all Christians who sacrificed their lives spreading the Good News.

It's a huge deal—our soul going to either heaven or hell after leaving this earthly body.

Think about, even though we live our best holiest life on this earthly, even for 120 years, we don't deserve living forever eternal heavenly life.

Also, even if someone lives the worst kind of life, doing evil for 120 years, an eternity torment in hell doesn't sounds fair either.

This means that after death, every one of us receives something we don't deserve.

If you believe in Jesus died for your sin, you get something incredibly good you don't deserve.

If you don't believe in Jesus, the father of lies will get you something horribly bad you don't deserve.

Please, ponder over this. Even though you don't believe heaven and hell, no one is absolutely sure. What if they are real...?!

At one point, we all be facing death, unavoidable accident. At that moment, that accident instantly sends us either to a glorious, joyful, peaceful heavenly retirement or a torturous, painful, agonizing hellish retirement—eternally.

Because of accidents, we pay for all kinds of insurance: auto insurance, fire insurance, health insurance, life insurance... you name it. We do it because we are not sure what might happen.

What if there really is heaven and hell? That would be the biggest issue of all. Even if there is an insurance company that offers a plan guaranteeing eternal heavenly retirement life forever—even for just 100 years—no one can afford the premiums.

That is where the Good News comes in. Jesus already paid the premium for our eternal heavenly retirement life. Paid in full. We don't need to pay a dime. So, everybody can afford—even the poorest person on earth has no excuse. All we need is to believe in our heart.

I thought about how to explain this...

Let's imagine a village where many poor people lived. All of them had borrowed large sums of money from a loan shark— dishonest and cruel man. He thrived on cheating, lying, and exploiting the poor, demanding high weekly interest payments and treating them like slaves.

One day, a kind and wealthy man with a compassionate heart heard how cruelly the poor villagers were being treated by the loan shark. Moved with pity, he went to the loan shark taking a few debtors with him as witnesses and paid off all the debts of the entire poor people. And the wealthy man turned to the witnesses and said, "Go and tell the others that their debts were fully paid. They are all free now." Then he returned to his home.

Now, with excitement, the witnesses went about and told the other poor people that their debts were paid. And some believed and rejoiced in their freedom and praised the wealthy man. But some refused to believe... saying there wouldn't be a person like that who would pay for their debt and continued to live as though they are still in debt, even though their debts were truly paid off...!

And the dishonest loan shark still roaming around the village demanding the poor people to pay interest taking a chance some might not yet know that their debts have been paid.

Those who believed the witnesses confronted the loan shark, "What are you talking about? I know my debt was paid by the generous wealthy man. So leave us alone. You don't have anything to do with us anymore." Then the loan shark leaves muttering, "Oh, they knew."

But the others who didn't believe kept paying interest, remaining under the loan shark's cruelty. He would continue exploiting them, collecting unjustly, as long as they don't find out.

How sad...! All he had to do is believe and proclaim.

Many people didn't just refuse to believe the good news—they even persecuted and killed those who spread the good news...!!

Another Astonishing Thing

Here is another astonishing thing; once we believe Jesus as our savior—we become children of God, the King of kings…!

That means I am now a princess…!

If someone not treating us well, that is because they don't know who we really are. So don't be upset. If they don't change the way they treat us, leave it to our Father, He will take of it.

I remember, long time ago, someone wronged me really big time while I liked and treated them well. After they did unspeakable thing to me, whenever I thought about them, I felt a little bitter. Not a lot. And every time when I thought about them with that bitterness, God made me feel so uncomfortable. So, I had to stop and couldn't keep thinking about them. And one day, I became frustrated with Him interrupting me again when they came into my thought. So, I talked to God, "Daddy, you know what they did to me. You saw it all...! And I am just thinking about what they did, not doing anything to pay them back...!!"

And you know what? The moment I finished my reasoning, God told me, "Inna, if you can hurt them without hurting yourself, do it by yourself...!" I was so shock that God doesn't want me to be hurt, even tiny bit. Even though I kit them with my hand, I am going to hurt my palm. And my Father doesn't want me to get hurt—even a tiny bit.

That day, I knew how much God loves me and soon I handed them over to God and later, God led me to forgive them and even praying for them. That doesn't mean I restore the relationship with them. No. To do that, they need to say, "Sorry" for what they did.

Also, what I found, while talking and asking God so many big and little things, even though God has so many gazillion children, He is capable of treating each one of us as His only child...! He is never busy to spend time talking with me. Actually, God enjoys spending time with me—lots of times with witty humorous remarks making me laugh a lot. And lots of time, when I talk about seemingly hard to handle problems with Him, while talking the problems turn to easy to handle and some were not even problems at all. I was just wasting my time and energy.

My love for Him becomes deeper and profound. How can you not...!?

Another thing I found that God want His children to bear the 9 fruits of the Holy Spirit (Galatians 5:22-23) as many as we can and as big as we can.

And with every obstacle, rejection, failure makes the fruits of the holy spirit in me becomes mature little by little...!

Fruits of the Holy Spirit include "Love": Love, joy, peace, forbearance, kindness, goodness, faithfulness, gentleness and self-control. (1 Corinthians 13:4-7)

I thought about all these traits, and found we can achieve anything with these traits...!

So, pick something grand at good one and work at it with the fruits of the holy spirit. Surely, there you will meet many obstacles: despair, failures, rejections, bankrupts... whatever. Work through them, if you can't, work around them. Just don't ever give up. You will succeed.

Colonel Sander's recipe was rejected for 1,009 times before starting KFC. The Star buck's founder, Howard Schultz, went through 217 rejections from lenders for a loan. And "Chicken Soup for the Soul was rejected by 144 publishers.

You can find out most people, if not all, who became very successful all went through many obstacles but never gave up.
By the way, did you know what Mary's last words in the Bible?

She said, "Do whatever He (Jesus) tells you." (John 2:5)

Mary was described as, "Highly favored." (Luke 1:28) by the angel Gabriel, and Mary said, "I am the Lord's servant." (Luke 1: 38) in the Bible.

Also, though people called Mary as Jesus' mother, Jesus never called Mary, "Mother." He called her, "Woman."

Jesus is "God" in flesh. ..!!!

"And You will know the Truth, and the Truth will Set You Free." (John 8:32)

What is the Truth?
Something that never going to change.